James M. Varnum

A Sketch of the Life and Public Services of James Mitchell

Varnum

of Rhode Island

James M. Varnum

A Sketch of the Life and Public Services of James Mitchell Varnum
of Rhode Island

ISBN/EAN: 9783337380984

Printed in Europe, USA, Canada, Australia, Japan

Cover: Foto ©Andreas Hilbeck / pixelio.de

More available books at **www.hansebooks.com**

A SKETCH

OF THE

LIFE AND PUBLIC SERVICES

OF

JAMES MITCHELL VARNUM

OF RHODE ISLAND,

Brigadier-General of the Continental Army; Member of the Continental Congress; Judge U. S. Supreme Court, N. W. Territory; Major-General Rhode Island Volunteer Militia.

By JAMES MITCHELL VARNUM,

Of New York City.

BOSTON :
DAVID CLAPP & SON, PRINTERS.
1906.

JAMES MITCHELL VARNUM.[5]

By James Mitchell Varnum.[6]

JAMES MITCHELL VARNUM, eldest son of Major Samuel Varnum, was born at Dracutt, Mass., on December 17th, 1748. After an academical education he entered Harvard College as a Freshman at the age of 16 years and 7 months, in the class of 1769, but did not continue there until graduation. There is no official record at the University as to the reason for his leaving Harvard, but inasmuch as in Quincy's history of Harvard College there is mention of disturbances amongst the students in April, 1768, in consequence of which some were rusticated and others expelled, it is considered probable that Varnum, who had the reputation of being rather "wild" at college, may have been one of the number.

He taught school in his native town of Dracutt in 1767, and on May 23d, 1768, entered Rhode Island College (now Brown University), from which institution he graduated with honors in 1769, in the first class to graduate from that college. At the "commencement" day celebration, which was held in the then new Baptist meeting-house at Warren, on September 7th, 1769, Varnum took a prominent place in the exercises, taking part in "a Syllogistic Disputation in Latin," and also being one of two students engaged in a "Forensic Dispute" entitled "The Americans in their present circumstances cannot consistent with good policy affect to become an independent state."

Mr. Varnum "ingeniously defended the proposition by cogent arguments handsomely dressed, though he was subtly, but delicately, opposed by Mr. William Williams, both of whom spoke with emphasis and propriety." Full copies of their

4

arguments may be found in Dr. Guild's account of the commencement.* As a sign of the times it may be mentioned that at this commencement "not only the candidates, but even the President, were dressed in American manufactures." †

In 1769, Mr. Varnum, after leaving college, again taught school for a time at Dracutt, but even at this early date seems to have decided to make his future home in Rhode Island, for soon thereafter he entered the office of the Honorable Oliver Arnold, Attorney General of the colony, with whom he was a student at law until the latter's decease in October, 1770.

It is probable, however, that young Varnum's decision to settle in Rhode Island was chiefly due to the fact that during his student life at Warren he had fallen in love with a fair daughter of that colony, whom he married on February 2d, 1770. Her name was Martha (usually known as Patty) Child, the eldest daughter of the Honorable Cromel Child of Warren, a member of the Rhode Island General Assembly, and one of a family of considerable, and even notable, distinction in those days.

One of her sisters married Hon. Benjamin Bourne, afterwards Member of Congress and United States District and Circuit Judge, and another Dr. Peter Turner, a distinguished surgeon in the Continental Army, and a prominent citizen of Rhode Island.

It may be here stated that Mr. Varnum's marriage proved to be a most happy one, he being represented by the chroniclers of that period as an "excellent and affectionate husband," and his consort as a "high-minded lady, and one of the most cheerful, sociable, and best of wives." Mrs. Varnum survived her husband 48 years, and died at Bristol, R. I., on October 10th, 1837, without issue, at the advanced age of 88 years.

* "The First Commencement of Rhode Island College," by R. A. Guild, Collection R. I. Historical Society, vol. 7. Providence, 1885.
† Manning and Brown University, by R. A. Guild. Gould & Lincoln, Boston, 1864.

In 1771, Mr. Varnum was admitted to the Bar, and soon after settled in East Greenwich, R. I., where his decided ability early acquired for him an extensive practice, and he travelled the circuit of the colony, reaping in an unusual degree for one so young the honors and pecuniary rewards of his profession. Mr. Wilkins Updyke, in his "Memoirs of the Rhode Island Bar," in referring to Mr. Varnum at this period of his life, says: "He was deeply attached to mathematical science, and delighted in its pursuit; his whole life was an evidence that he was naturally a mathematician; his habits were those of intense study and boisterous relaxation. He was fond of exhibiting his skill in gymnastics, and ever ready to exercise in that ancient art with any one who would engage with him, noble or ignoble. Strong and active in frame, and ardently attached to such exercises, he gave his inclination for such sports the fullest range to a late period in his life." In another portion of his biography of General Varnum, and referring generally to his character, Mr. Updyke says: "Varnum was periodically an intense student, and would be secluded for weeks. He possessed the rare power of great mental abstraction and philosophic ratiocination. He was master of his cases, and all the facts were well arranged and digested for trial. Varnum told a friend that he studied his cases in bed, and often had his books brought to him. This is the solution of the mystery which some thought was intuition, of instantly rising in court and arguing his cause, to public surprise and admiration, without any apparent previous preparation or consultation. He was a great admirer of Vattel and Montesquieu; the latter he would almost repeat. He delighted in, and cultivated his taste for, the poets. Shakespeare, Young, Pope, and Addison he would recite with great readiness, and when a novel came into his hands his meals were suspended until it was finished."

It was about this time, on August 15th, 1773, that Mr. Varnum purchased for £18. the land at East Greenwich upon which he commenced the erection of the colonial mansion, to which reference will hereafter be made. Owing, however, to the troubled condition of the country, and the war which soon followed, in which Mr. Varnum took such an interested and active part, his building operations were interrupted, and the house was not completed and occupied until some four or five years thereafter.

Mr. Varnum, very early in life, took an intense and active interest in military affairs, especially in view of the discontent in the colonies with the rule of Great Britain, and his firm conviction that sooner or later war must ensue. He made a careful study not only of military tactics, but also of the art and science of war, which afterwards stood him in good stead.

In October, 1774, he became a charter member and the commander, with the rank of Colonel, of the Kentish Guards, a uniformed militia company of infantry in East Greenwich, then chartered by the Rhode Island General Assembly under the style of the "First Independent Company of the County of Kent," and which subsequently gave 32 commissioned officers to the army of the American Revolution, amongst them Gen. Nathaniel Greene, Gen. Varnum, Col. Christopher Greene, Col. Crary and Maj. Whitmarsh.

It was about this time, and in connection with the Kentish Guards, that there began that intimacy and devoted friendship that existed between Nathaniel Greene and James M. Varnum until they were parted by the death of the latter.

Mr. George Washington Greene, in his life of Maj.-Gen. Greene, after alluding to Greene's deep interest in the Kentish Guards, says:—

"Amongst the first officers was James M. Varnum, a man of 'exalted talents,' whom he 'loved and esteemed,' who was to take an honorable place in the civil and military history of the Revolution.

Nathaniel Greene was only a private in the company, but subsequently became a candidate for a lieutenancy, a candidature which met with considerable opposition.

Greene, it seems, had had a trouble with one of his knees, which gave a slight limp to his gait, and in the eyes of some of the village and company critics, this limp, although slight, was a serious blemish, unfitting him not merely for an officer, but even for a private.

Greene was thunderstruck at this opposition, and took it sorely to heart. His friends were indignant. Varnum threatened to withdraw his name, and the loss of Varnum's fine person and popular eloquence would have been a serious blow to the half-organized company." *

How this matter was finally settled we know not, but doubtless Greene withdrew his candidacy for lieutenant, and persuaded his friends to agree to it, for he remained a private in the company until about two years later, when, over the heads of all his critics, he was promoted to a Brigadier-Generalcy by his fellow-members of the Rhode Island Legislature, an appointment which his subsequent brilliant career fully justified.

An interesting letter written by Greene to his friend and commander, Varnum, at the time of the above-mentioned trouble, is still extant,† and is worthy of preservation in this volume, although it has already been printed in full in the life of Gen. Greene, above referred to.

It is addressed to James M. Varnum, Esq., East Greenwich, and was probably written in the autumn of 1774, or early in 1775, and reads as follows:—

Coventry, Monday, 2 o'clock, p. m.

Dear Sir :—

As I am ambitious of maintaining a place in your esteem, and I cannot hope to do it, if I discover in my actions a little mind and a mean spirit I think in justice to myself I ought to acquaint you with the particulars of the subject upon which we conversed to-day—I was informed

---

* G. W. Greene's "History of General Greene," vol. 1, page 50.
† Original letter is in the possession of James M. Varnum of New York.

the gentlemen of East Greenwich said I was a blemish to the company—I confess it is the first stroke of mortification that I ever felt from being considered either in private or publick life a blemish to those with whom I associated—hitherto I have always had the happiness to find myself respected in society in general, and my friendship courted by as respectable characters as any in the Government—pleased with these thoughts, and anxious to promote the good of my country—and ambitious of increasing the consequence of East Greenwich—I have exerted myself to form a military company there—but little did I think that the Gentlemen considered me in the light of an obtruder—my heart is too susceptible of pride, and my sentiments too delicate to wish a connexion where I am considered in an inferior point of light—I have always made it my study to promote the interest of Greenwich and to cultivate the good opinion of its inhabitants, that the severity of speech and the union of sentiment, coming from persons so unexpected—might wound the pride of my heart deeper than the force of the observation merited—God knows when I first entered this company I had not in contemplation any kind of office, but was fully determined not to accept any, but Greff and others have been endeavouring to obtain my consent for some weeks past—I never expected that being a member of that company would give me any more consequence in life, either as private soldier or commissioned officer—I thought the cause of Liberty was in danger, and as it was attackt by a military force, it was necessary to cultivate a military spirit amongst the People, that should tyranny endeavor to make any further advances we might be prepared to check it in its first sallies. I considered with myself that if we never should be wanted in that character, it would form a pretty little society in our meetings, where we might relax ourselves a few hours from the various occupations of life—and return to our business again with more activity and spirit—I did not want to add any new consequence to myself from the distinction of that company—if I had been ambitious of promotion in a publick character—you yourself can witness for me I have had it in my power—but I always preferred the pleasures of private society to those of publick distinction—If I conceive aright of the force of the objection of the gentlemen of the town it was not as an officer, but as a soldier, for that my halting was a blemish to the rest—I confess it is my misfortune to limp a little, but I did not conceive it to be so great, but we are not apt to discover our own defects. I feel the less mortified at it as it's

9

natural and not a stain or defection, that resulted from my actions—I have pleased myself with the thoughts of serving under you, but as it is the general opinion that I am unfit for such an undertaking I shall desist—I feel not the less inclination to promote the good of the Company because I am not to be one of its members—I will do any thing that's in my power to procure the Charter, I will be at my proportion of the expense until the company is formed and completly equipt—Let me entreat you, Sir, if you have any regard for me, not to forsake the company at this crititical season for I fear the consequences—if you mean to oblige me by it, I assure you it will not, I would not have the company break and disband for fifty Dollars—it would be a disgrace upon the county and upon the town in particular. I feel more mortification than resentment—but I think it would have manifested a more generous temper to have given me their opinions in private than to make proclamation of it in publick as a capital objection, for nobody loves to be the subject of ridicule however true the cause—I purpose to attend to-morrow if my business will permit—and as Mr. Greene is waiting will add no more only that I am with great truth

Your sincere friend,

NATHANAEL GREENE.

The prominent part taken by Varnum in the Colonial controversy inspired him with an ambition to enter the military service of his country, and when the news of the battle of Lexington reached East Greenwich, in 1775, Col. Varnum assembled the Kentish Guards, and within three hours, well uniformed, armed and equipped, they were on the march to Providence, and thence to Pawtucket, where they learned that the enemy had retired to Boston, and that their services were no longer required. The next week the General Assembly of Rhode Island authorized the raising of a brigade of three regiments of infantry, under Nathaniel Greene, then a member of the Assembly, as Brigadier-General, and Varnum was selected as Colonel of the regiment to be raised in the counties of Kent and Kings, and on May 8th, 1775, he was commissioned by the Provincial General Assembly as Colonel of the

1st Regiment Rhode Island Infantry in the Brigade of Observation. After the 5th of August of that year the regiment
was known as the 12th Continental Foot, and during the year
1776 officially designated the 9th Continental Foot. When
this first change in name took place the officers received commissions from the President of Congress, when Washington
was appointed commander-in-chief, and their commands were
then styled Continental troops.

On the 8th of June, 1775, Col. Varnum arrived with his
regiment at Roxbury, and reported to Brig.-Gen. Greene.
Here it was under fire during the shelling of that place on the
17th of June, 1775, and also at Plowed Hill on August 26th.
During the cannonade at the last-named place Adjt. Mumford
and another member of the regiment had their heads shot off.

On the 23d July, the Rhode Island Brigade removed to
Prospect Hill. Col. Varnum's regiment continued at the siege
of Boston until the town was evacuated by the enemy, 17th
of March, 1776. Meanwhile the terms of service of most of the
enlisted men had expired in December, but they continued on
duty until the 1st of January, 1776, and then almost all re-
enlisted for another year.

Marching from Boston on the 1st of April, 1776, the regiment went into temporary quarters at Providence, and then
proceeded via Norwich to New London, where it embarked in
transports for New York City, and arrived there on the 17th
of April.

Pursuant to general orders from Army Headquarters, New
York, 30th April, 1776, the 1st and 2nd Rhode Island Continental Infantry crossed the East River to Brooklyn on the 3rd
of May and began to fortify the heights.

On the 1st of June, pursuant to Brig.-Gen. Nathaniel
Greene's orders of that date from Brooklyn Heights, five companies of Col. Varnum's regiment were stationed upon the right

in Fort Box, and the other three between that work and Fort
Greene.

On the 9th of June, Brig.-Gen. Greene directed the 1st and
2nd Rhode Island and Col. Moses Little's 12th regiment Continental Foot (8th Mass. Infantry) of his brigade to exercise
together four days in each week.

On the 17th of June, Brig.-Gen. Greene assigned six companies of Col. Varnum's regiment to garrison Fort Box, which
was near the line of the present Pacific Street, a short distance
above Bond Street, Brooklyn, and two companies to the
"Oblong" redoubt, which was on a piece of rising ground at
the corner of the present De Kalb and Hudson Avenues,
Brooklyn.

On the 8th of July, the same general officer ordered the 1st
Rhode Island, Col. Varnum, to go and garrison Fort Defiance,
at Red Hook, Brooklyn, which in a communication to Gen.
Washington from Headquarters, Brooklyn Heights, 5th July,
he said he regarded as "a post of vast importance."

Here the regiment remained during the battle of Long
Island, on the extreme right flank of Maj.-Gen. Israel Putnam's forces, engaged with the allied British and Hessian
forces, and nearest to the enemy's ships.

On the 30th of August, the 1st and 2nd Rhode Island having evacuated the lines, re-crossed the East River to the City
of New York early in the morning.

In the action at Harlem Heights, the regiment was an active
participant under its Lieut.-Col. (Archibald Crary), Col. Varnum being at the time on the sick report.

Soon afterward the regiment crossed the Hudson at Fort
Lee, and was there on the 23d of September with the remainder of the brigade (Nixon's, late Greene's), which included
the 2nd Rhode Island. From thence, on the 13th of October,
pursuant to Brig.-Gen. John Nixon's orders of that date and

place, which he had issued in compliance with Maj.-Gen. Greene's instructions, the brigade immediately moved over the ferry to Fort Washington, and on the 16th of October was at East Chester, from whence, on that date, Col. Varnum's regiment was ordered to march toward Throg's Neck, at the entrance of Long Island Sound, where the British had landed on the 12th, and to retard their advance. Taking post at the west end of the causeway from Throg's Neck, with a detachment at Westchester Mill, on the causeway where the bridge planks had been removed, the 1st Rhode Island remained here until the 18th, and then moved to Valentine's Hill.

Two days later, Col. Varnum was with his regiment at the battle of White Plains, and on the 1st of November in camp at North Castle. On the 22nd of November, the regiment was quartered near Phillipsburg, and crossed the Hudson with the brigade on the 2nd of December, and was at Haverstraw on the 4th of December.

As the terms of service of the several Rhode Island Continental regiments were drawing to a close, he here left his regiment, and was sent by his Excellency, the commander-in-chief, to Rhode Island, to hasten, by his influence and presence, the recruitment of the army.

On the 12th of October preceding, Gen. Washington, from Army Headquarters, Harlem Heights, had specially recommended him for retention in the army on its proposed re-arrangement " for the war."

He had been at home but a few days when the Rhode Island General Assembly appointed him on the 12th of December, 1776, Brigadier-General of the State Militia, and also of the Rhode Island State Brigade on the Continental Establishment. He relinquished his regimental commission on acceptance of this last commission, and was on duty successively at Tiverton 8th, 23rd January, and 11th to 17th March, 1777, Providence 25th

January, Warren 12th March, South Kingston 20th April, and Exeter 24th May, 1777. He was appointed Brigadier-General of the Continental Army 21st of February, 1777, and notified thereof by Gen. Washington in complimentary terms from Army Headquarters, Morristown, N. J., 3rd of March, 1777. Gen. Washington's letter contains ample evidence that his military record and bearing had met with the full approbation of the distinguished commander-in-chief. This new appointment vacated that under which he was then acting, and the Rhode Island General Assembly at the March session, 1777, passed a resolution on the subject "in grateful remembrance of his services."

Using his personal influence, which was great, to hasten re-enlistment and the recruitment of the 1st and 2nd Rhode Island Continentals, after their return in February from Morristown, N. J., he was enabled on the 8th of April to send forward to that place to join the "main" army a detachment from each, under Lieut.-Col. Jeremiah Olney. Under Gen. Washington's instructions from Army Headquarters at the last-named place, of the 11th of May, the two regiments when they did leave Rhode Island were directed to march to Peekskill, in the Middle Department, then under Maj.-Gen. Israel Putnam. They arrived there on or about the 23rd of May, and were at first quartered in Peekskill. Brig.-Gen. Varnum personally arrived about the 1st of June. On the 12th of June, Gen. Washington, in consequence of a movement of the enemy, directed from Army Headquarters, Middlebrook, Maj.-Gen. Putnam to forward to that place a portion of his forces. This detachment included Varnum's Brigade. While with the "main army" his brigade, on the 22nd of June, 1777, formed part of the forces detached under Maj.-Gen. Nathaniel Greene to make a demonstration against the enemy in New Brunswick. In this successful movement against Sir William Howe, Varnum's Brigade marched down on the west side of the Raritan and followed the retreating enemy several miles toward Amboy. On the 1st of July, the brigade was ordered back by his Excellency, the commander-in-chief, and on the 2nd of July marched from Middlebrook.

The 1st Rhode Island was then sent to Maj.-Gen. Putnam to garrison Fort Montgomery.

On the 20th of August, pursuant to the latter's orders from Department Headquarters, Peckskill, Brig.-Gen. Varnum left that place on special service with a detachment to White Plains, from whence the 2nd Rhode Island went nearly to King's Bridge, in the "neutral ground" of Westchester County.

The expedition was successful, and incidentally captured two subalterns and several enlisted men of the enemy.

It returned to Peekskill on the 26th.

On the 23d September, General Washington, from Army Headquarters in camp near Pottsgrove, Pa., instructed Maj.-Gen. Putnam to send a certain detachment of troops to him without delay, via Morristown.

Accordingly the 4th Regt. Conn. Cont'l Inf'y (Col. John Durkee) and the 8th Regt. Conn. Cont'l Inf'y (Col. John Chandler) were added to Brig.-Gen. Varnum's brigade, and it again crossed the Hudson River. It arrived at Caryell's Ferry on the Delaware on the 7th October, and here he was directed to halt, and by orders of the 7th October to detach the 1st and 2d Rhode Island to Fort Mercer. Soon afterwards, he moved to Woodbury, N. J., where Brigade Headquarters were established.

On the 1st Nov., 1777, Gen. Washington, from Army Headquarters Whitemarsh, directed him to take supervision of Fort Mercer, Red Bank, and of Fort Mifflin, Mud Island, and relieve Lt.-Col. Samuel Smith, 4th Maryland Cont'l Inf'y, the commandment of Fort Mifflin, who had requested to be relieved on the 18th October.

However, in prospect of an attack, Lt.-Col. Smith was continued in command, and exercised it on the 10 Nov. when the firing was resumed, until the afternoon of the 11th, when he was severely wounded in the arm and left the fort. Brig.-Gen. Varnum, then at Fort Mercer, immediately detailed Lieut.-Col. Giles Russell, 8th Conn., who went over and assumed command, and relieved part of the garrison by a detachment from his own, the 4th Conn. (Col. John Durkee's).

On the 12th, Lieut.-Col. Russell, ill and exhausted by fatigue, asked to be relieved, and while Brig.-Gen. Varnum was considering what field officer to detail to the hazardous duty, Maj. Simeon Thayer, 2d Rhode Island, volunteered, and went over and relieved Lieut.-Col. Russell and the remainder of Lieut.-Col. Smith's men with a detachment of Rhode Islanders.

As the land defences of the Delaware had been entrusted by Gen. Washington to Brig.-Gen. Varnum, the anxiety of the latter to fulfil his whole duty with the inadequate force under him was extreme.

During the bombardment of Fort Mifflin and its heroic defence on the 15th Nov., 1777, he reported to Gen. Washington at 6 P.M., as follows: "We have lost a great many men to-day; a great many officers are killed and wounded. My fine company of artillery is almost destroyed. We shall be obliged to evacuate the fort this night."

After the two forts were evacuated he marched his brigade, 20th November, to Mount Holly and joined Maj.-Gen. Greene's division there a few days later.

Having crossed the Delaware, his brigade joined the main army at Whitemarsh about the 29th Nov., and was in the operations in that vicinity against Sir William Howe's army, 5th–8th December.

Proceeding with his brigade to Valley Forge on the 19th Dec., it there erected huts and went into winter quarters.* The brigade of General Varnum was stationed on a hill where a star redoubt was erected, whence an extensive view of both sides of the Schuylkill River could be secured, and so near the steam as to be able to employ the artillery to check any attempt of the enemy to cross over near the place, but their use for that purpose was never required. The redoubt was about 1½ miles from Washington's headquarters; and just within the lines and a short distance beyond were the headquarters of General Varnum, at the residence of David Stevens, the next farm house below that occupied by Washington. This house is still standing, and has recently been described, as follows: "The house is of stone with a long porch facing the road, and is quite remarkable for the thickness of the western wall—about 12 feet. The ceilings are low, and there is a general appearance of comfort surrounding it. The main room has still the large old open fire place. It is situate close to the River road, and about three hundred feet from the ruins of the Star Redoubt, which was the strongest of the works at Valley Forge, commanding the road and the river for miles, and was doubtless the key to the situation."†

The trials, sufferings and privations of the Continental Army at Valley Forge are too well known to all students of history to require any extended allusion thereto, and the same may be said as to the bitter attacks and cabals against General Washington at this time, but the following extracts from letters of General Varnum may be of interest. On December 22d, 1777, he wrote to General Washington, as follows:

---

* History of Valley Forge, by Henry Woodman (collection of Penn. Hist. Society). Also John F. Watrous' memo. in same collection.

† J. V. P. Turner, Esq., of Philadelphia, in Newport Mercury, Dec. 21st, 1895; and in personal correspondence with the Editors, 1902.

" According to the saying of Solomon, hunger will break through a stone wall. It is therefore a very pleasing circumstance to the Division under my command that there is probability of their marching. Three days successively have we been destitute of bread. Two days we have been entirely without meat. The men must be supplied or they cannot be commanded. The complaints are too urgent to pass unnoticed. It is with pain that I mention this distress. I know that it will make your Excellency unhappy; but if you expect the exertion of virtuous principle while your troops are deprived of the necessaries of life, your final disappointment will be great in proportion to the patience which now astonishes every man of human feeling."*

In a letter to his life long friend, General Nathaniel Greene, dated Valley Forge, Feb. 1st, 1778, he speaks of General Washington, as follows:

"I know the great General in this as in all his other measures, acts from goodness of soul and with a view only to the public weal. * * * You have often heard me say, and, I assure you, I feel happy in the truth of it, that next to God Almighty, and my country, I revere General Washington, and nothing fills me with so much indignation as the villany of some who dare speak disrespectfully of him."

On February 16, 1778, General Varnum wrote another letter from camp to General Greene, as follows:

"The situation of the camp is such that in all human probability the army must soon dissolve. Many of the troops are destitute of meat and are several days in arrear. The horses are dying for want of forage. The country in the vicinity of the camp is exhausted. * * * * My freedom upon this occasion may be offensive; if so I should be unhappy, but duty compels me to speak without reserve."†

General Varnum was the first person in the country to advocate the enlistment of negroes as soldiers, and thus to recog-

* Ford's Washington, vol. 6, page 254.
† Ford's Washington, vol. 6, page 381.

nize courage "behind a thatch of wool." On January 2d, 1778, in view of the difficulty of obtaining sufficient troops for the Continental Army, he suggested to General Washington the propriety of raising a battalion of negroes to make up the proportion of Rhode Island in the army. Washington submitted this suggestion to the executive of Rhode Island without approval or disapproval. The Rhode Island Legislature, however, promptly passed an act authorizing the enlistment in two battalions of negroes and Indians; every slave enlisting to receive his freedom, and his owner to be paid by the State an amount not exceeding £125. At least one battalion was successfully raised, and did excellent service at the battle of Rhode Island.*

General Varnum seems to have been one of the most aggressive and strenuous of the general officers of the army in presenting, not only to the Commander-in-Chief, but also to the State of Rhode Island and to Congress, the sufferings and needs of the Continental troops at Valley Forge, and in demanding some immediate relief for them, and doubtless this aggressiveness and insistence led him naturally to incur the hostility of some active members of the general government, for on May 23d, 1778, Governeur Morris, then a member of Congress from New York, writes to Washington concerning Varnum that his "temper and manners are by no means calculated to teach Patience, Discipline and Subordination." †

Dr. William Shaw Bowen says of Varnum :

"His talents for the conduct of business affairs were very great, and his manners were so engaging that Varnum was called on by Washington to conduct delicate negotiations for the Continental as well as for the State Government. Washington placed a high estimate on him."

"The solemn visage of the father of his country must have relaxed when

* Ford's Washington, vol. 6, page 347.
† Ford's Washington, Vol. 7, p. 30.

he referred to him as 'the light of the camp' during the dreadful winter at Valley Forge."*

Pursuant to General Washington's orders dated Army Headquarters Valley Forge, 7th May, 1778, he was directed under the resolution of Congress of the 3d February preceding, to administer the oath of office to the officers of his own and Brig.-Genl. Jedediah Huntington's brigade of Connecticut Continental Infantry.

On the 4th March, 4th, 23d, and 29th April, 17th, 26th and 28th of May and 4th June, he was Brigadier-General of the day to the "Main" Army at Valley Forge. Soon afterward and before the evacuation of Philadelphia by the enemy, he went on special duty to Rhode Island. Here his brigade joined him near Providence on the 3d August, 1778, preparatory to the campaign before Newport. It now consisted, under General orders dated Army Hd. Qrs. Wright's Mills, 22d July, 1778, of the 2d R. I. Contl. Infantry (Col. Israel Angell), Colonels Henry Sherburne's and Saml. B. Webb's additional Regts. Contl. Infy. and the 1st Regt. Canadian Contl. Infy. (Col. James Livingston).

On the 14th August pursuant to Genl. Orders of Maj.-Genl. John Sullivan dated Hd. Qrs. Portsmouth, R.I., he was assigned to the command of the right wing of the front line of the Army in Rhode Island, and by the same authority was directed to command the covering party in the lines at the siege of Newport on the 16th.

In addition to his other duties he was detailed as President of a General Court Martial, per Major-General Sullivan's orders, dated Hd. Qrs. before Newport, 17th Aug., 1778, and continued on this duty until the 29th August when the Court was dissolved.

* *Providence Journal*, March 6th, 1902. [This remark was made by Washington to Captain Samuel Packard of Providence (grandfather of Dr. Bowen), and frequently repeated by Capt. Packard.]

On the 14th and 31st August he was Brigadier of the Day to the Army.

In the battle of Rhode Island his command bore the principal part of the fighting against the forces of Maj.-Genl. Robt. Pigot.

In General Orders dated Hd. Qrs. Department of R. I., Tiverton, 31st Aug., 1778, his brigade was ordered "to take post at Bristol and Warren, divided as he shall think best for the defence of those posts." He made his Brigade Hd. Qrs. at Warren until 26th Feby., 1779, when he was at East Greenwich. Meanwhile Major-General Sullivan, during his own absence, by General Orders dated Hd. Qrs. Providence, 27th January, 1779, placed him temporarily in command of the Department of Rhode Island.

The necessity of attending to his private affairs, and to the support and maintenance of his family, compelled him at this time much against his will to tender his resignation to Congress. In a letter to his friend, Genl. Greene, dated 26th Feby., 1779, he says: "The resolution was painful, but hard necessity urged it by every cogent motive." He was honorably discharged from the service "at his own request," 5th March, 1779.

Upon official notification of acceptance of his resignation, Maj. General John Sullivan, in Genl. Orders Hd. Qrs. Department of Rhode Island, Providence, 18th March, 1779, said:

"Brigadier-General Varnum having this day notified the Commander-in-Chief that he has transmitted a final resignation of his commission to Congress, and that he is under the disagreeable necessity of quitting the service of the United States:

The General esteems it his duty to return his sincere and most cordial thanks to Brig.-Genl. Varnum for his brave, spirited and soldierlike conduct while acting under his immediate command in this Department, and sincerely laments that an officer, who by his conduct, has merited so much from the public, should be under the disagreeable necessity of leaving a service where his exertions as an officer would have been of essential advantage had he been able to continue in the army."

Appointed by the R. I. General Assembly to be Major-General R. I. Militia, 5th May, 1779, he continued in this office by unanimous annual reappointments until the 7th May, 1788, and was, from the 25th July to the 8th Aug., 1780, called into the actual service of the United States under Lieut.-Genl. the Comte de Rochambeau. On the 26th Oct., 1779, he was appointed by the Rhode Island General Assembly Advocate in the State Court of Admiralty.

Upon his resignation from the army General Varnum returned to his home at East Greenwich, completed the construction of his dwelling and resumed the active practice of the law.

As to this house of General Varnum's, which is still standing (1906), and in excellent preservation, although more than a century and a quarter old, we have an interesting description in an article written by its present owner and occupant, Dr. William Shaw Bowen, which was published in the *Providence Journal* of March 6th, 1892, from which we quote as follows:

"Of the pre-revolutionary mansions there are few better specimens in existence than the Varnum place in East Greenwich. The venerable edifice has been shielded from the approaches of the iconoclastic 'restorer,' and today, in its interior, it is one of the most perfect of the remaining instances of colonial architecture the country affords. In its way it is as unique as the Braddock house at Alexandria, Va., the Chancellor Wythe mansion at Williamsburg, or the Brandon place on the James River near Richmond. Varnum house is not only rich in the perfect details of its kind, but it teems with historic interest. Few houses in Rhode Island are more replete with associations of the last days of her colonial history and the early period of independent existence, the hiatus between the date of the separation from English rule and that of the final union with the established States of the American Union.

＊　　　＊　　　＊　　　＊　　　＊　　　＊

The present owner cherishes the home of the brilliant and versatile Varnum, and takes pride in preserving the old place in its original style. The hall, which closely resembles that of the Vernon house, is wainscoted on the first and second floors, as are nearly all of the rooms. The woodwork of the parlor is greatly admired by architects. The heavy cornice is dentated and the pediment above the fireplace is peculiarly graceful in its effect. The doors have small, oval, fluted brass knobs. All of the rooms have open fireplaces with tile facings. The fireplace of the dining room is seven feet in width and constructed of cut granite. The rooms are filled with antique black mahogany furniture, mostly of the Georgian age. The parlor set was brought from England in the last century."

In the same article we find a picturesque and attractive account of a visit paid by the Marquis de Lafayette and a party of French officers in September, 1778, to General Varnum at his East Greenwich home. It reads as follows :

"On a warm afternoon in September, in the year 1778, a small sloop rounded 'the rocks,' which jut out into Coweset Bay from the estate now occupied as a summer residence by William Stoddard, Esq., of Providence. The fresh southerly breeze which prevails a considerable portion of the year wafted the craft to Long Point, which limits the little Greenwich cove. Then the sloop made a few tacks, and was speedily tied alongside the wharf at the foot of King Street. The loungers on shore, attracted by the new arrival, beheld a gallant spectacle on the sloop's deck. There was a handsome young man clad in the buff and blue regimentals of a general officer in the Continental army. He was of medium height, erect and dignified, and his manners were those of one who is in a position to command men. With distinguished courtesy he assisted several unknown military gentlemen to the shore. The uniform worn by the strangers was unfamiliar to the barefooted youths who clustered on the caplog of the wharf. It consisted of a green coat faced with red and laced with gold. The breeches were of buff cloth. Black silk stockings, a four-cornered cocked hat and a large red silk sash were other features of the costume. One of the number was clad in the Continental blue and buff. On him the attention of the first mentioned officer were especially bestowed. He ' was a young man with sharp features and a prominent nose. When the shore was reached the first officer in Continental uniform exclaimed : 'My dear Marquis, welcome to East Greenwich and my home.'

The speaker was Brigadier-General James Mitchell Varnum, who commanded a brigade at the battle fought on Rhode Island on August 29th previous between the American army under General Sullivan and the British garrison at Newport. His guest was the Marquis de La Fayette, who was sent with two brigades of Continental troops by Washington to reinforce Sullivan. The failure of the French fleet to coöperate compelled Sullivan to evacute Rhode Island after the sanguinary contest of Butts Hill and Quaker Hill. The officers in green were Frenchmen. They came to the county seat of Kent to partake of Gen. Varnum's hospitality.

The record of what transpired during the stay of La Fayette rests wholly on the reminiscences of the late Miss Eleanor Fry, a venerable Quakeress who lived in an ancient gambrel-roofed house on the site now occupied by the Central Hotel, immediately adjoining the Kent County Court House on the south. Miss Fry, known to the villagers as 'Cousin Ellen,' died many years ago. She was a beautiful woman in her youth, and a favorite in the courtly society of the Revolutionary period. She witnessed the little procession of guests léd by Gen. Varnum with La Fayette at his side as they came along King Street, crossed Main Street and thence walked up the short ascent of Court Street—by the house afterwards occupied by Dr. Peter Turner of Continental army fame at the battle of Red Bank—to the residence of Gen. Varnum on Pearce Street.

The imposing façade of the house appeared exactly as at present, save that it was not shadowed by the two great elm trees that stand in front. They were then young trees recently planted. The location was, as it is today, the best in the village. Narragansett Bay stretched out in front toward Newport. Warwick Neck and distant Bristol were in view. The quaint old town, then consisting almost entirely of unpainted houses, the streets sandy and rain-washed, lay on the side hill sloping toward the waters of Greenwich Cove. In 1778 the Varnum mansion was isolated, with broad fields and meadows on either side and extending far back in the rear. Pearce Street contained only four houses, and was an out-of-the-way portion of the village. The house, resplendent with white paint, green blinds, and huge, shining brass knocker on the front door, was regarded as a palace by the townspeople, many of whom characterized it as 'Varnum's Folly,' and as savoring of aristocratic and unrepublican pretense and display.

According to 'Cousin Ellen' Fry the several days that the gallant La Fayette and the French officers passed as the guests of Gen. Varnum were of unwonted gayety. Every evening tea was served, to which the village beauties, with their chaperons, were invited. La Fayette lodged in the northeast chamber. His valet slept on a cot outside the door. Gen. Varnum occupied the southeast chamber. The French officers were placed in the southwest chamber. The nights were spent in conviviality. It was a free living, hard drinking age, and the breakfasts were at a very late hour.

The occasion of La Fayette's visit was characterized by Gen. Varnum as his *house-warming*. It is believed that Gen. Sullivan was of the memorable party.

Returning from a visit to Boston, Gen. Washington passed a night in Varnum's house. He dined and supped there, and during the afternoon enjoyed a brief siesta in the northeast chamber. The journey westward was resumed the following day over the old road through Coventry, to Lebanon, where Washington stayed with Governor Jonathan Trumbull."

Generals Nathanael Greene and John Sullivan and the Comte de Rochambeau, the Commander-in-Chief of the French army,—under whom Gen. Varnum served in Rhode Island, and between whom and Varnum there was formed a sincere and lasting friendship, with sundry members of his staff,—were also guests at this hospitable mansion.

Commissary General Claude Blanchard of the French army relates in his diary that when he dined with General Varnum, at the latter's house on the 20th of August, 1780, the entire conversation was carried on in Latin.

It was doubtless at or soon after the visit of the Marquis de Lafayette above referred to, that the latter presented to General Varnum the Punch Bowl, of which a picture appears in this volume, and which is now owned by the Rhode Island Society of the Cincinnati, of which General Varnum was subsequently President.

In April, 1780, the people of the State of Rhode Island "in

grateful recollection of his eminent services in the cause of public liberty, and desirous to throw into the national councils those distinguished talents which could be spared from the field," elected General Varnum their delegate to the Confederated or Continental Congress of that year, and he was reëlected the next year, serving from May 3d, 1780, to May 1, 1782; and he was subsequently reëlected for the term from May 1st, 1786, to May 2d, 1787.

As that body sat with closed doors, his voice could not be heard by the public, but his name appeared very often on the published journal, and it is evident that he exerted great power and influence.

In 1781 he was one of the Committee appointed to apportion amongst the States the assessments for public expenses and carrying on the war, was Chairman of the Committee to whom was referred a report of the Board of Admiralty, embracing instructions to private armed vessels, was one of the Committee who reported a resolution which was adopted giving the thanks of Congress to Brigadier-General Morgan and the officers and men under his command for their fortitude and good conduct in the action at the Cowpens.

In 1782 he served on many committees, and amongst others was Chairman of the Committee authorizing the exchange of Lieut.-General Burgoyne and his officers; he reported and had passed a resolution urging the States to send full representations to Congress; was on Committee to express the thanks of Congress to Washington, Rochambeau and de Grasse after the victory at Yorktown; and was Chairman of the Committee to thank General Greene and his officers after the battle of Eutaw Springs. In 1786-7 General Varnum also occupied similar important positions in Congress.

Mr. Augustus C. Buell, in his recently published work entitled "Paul Jones, founder of the American Navy" (Vol. II.

pp. 58–61) refers to General Varnum as the Chairman of the
Select Committee of Congress, March 28th, 1781, to investi-
gate and report as to the conduct of Commodore John Paul
Jones, which committee, after a protracted and searching inquiry, not only exonerated the Commodore from all charges,
but reported resolutions giving him the thanks of the United
States for his distinguished services, which resolutions were
unanimously passed by Congress by standing vote.

Mr. Buell also gives interesting quotations from General
Varnum's own account of the proceedings of that committee.*

It appears also that Varnum was one of a committee appointed by Congress to draft a proclamation which was adopted
and issued by Congress on the 26th day of October, 1781,
designating December 13th as a day of general thanksgiving
and prayer, in special commemoration of the confederation of
the States, the victories of our allies at sea, the prowess of our
troops, and the surrender of Cornwallis and his whole army at
Yorktown.

Those familiar with Varnum's writing and addresses are of
the opinion from the style and form of the proclamation that he
was its draughtsman.†

The distinguished Dr. William Samuel Johnson, of Connecticut, who was in Congress with him in 1786, referring to
General Varnum's Congressional career, said that "he was a
man of uncommon talents and of the most brilliant eloquence."

In the "Memoirs of Elkanah Watson," an exceedingly rare
book, may be found interesting details concerning Varnum.
The writer describes some of his characteristics :

"I first saw this learned and amiable man in 1774, when I heard him
deliver a Masonic oration. Until that moment I had formed no conception

* Memorial of James Mitchell Varnum. His publick services, and excerpts from his diary
of events printed for subscribers.—Providence, 1792.
† "Proclamation for Thanksgiving issued by the Continental Congress, &c."—Munsell &
Rowland, Albany, 1858.

of the power and charms of oratory. I was so deeply impressed that the effects of his splendid exhibition has remained for 48 years indelibly fixed on my mind. I then compared his mind to a beautiful parterre, from which he was enabled to pluck the most gorgeous and fanciful flowers, in his progress to enrich and embellish the subject."

General Varnum upon his retirement from the army devoted himself assiduously to the practice of the law, with increased reputation, and despite interruptions later for several years caused by his Congressional duties, became recognized as one of the leading and most brilliant men at the bar of Rhode Island, and was retained in all the most important causes.

Many great and important cases arose growing out of the relations of the nation to the state. One of the most notable of these, was the great paper money case of Trevett against Weeden, which stirred the community to its very foundation. The questions involved and their importance are fully set forth at considerable length in the biography of General Varnum in Undyke's Memoirs of the Rhode Island Bar. It was tried in September, 1786.

General Varnum was the counsel for the successful defendant, and his argument was considered masterly and convincing.

An attempt being afterwards made to impeach the Justices of the Supreme Court for their decision in the above case, General Varnum appeared for the judges, and his argument is described as having been "copious, argumentative and eloquent," and the attempt at impeachment fell through.

Mr. Updyke says, "It was eulogium enough on Varnum that the power of those speeches wrought such a triumphant victory over public opinion, that the dominant party, to save themselves from political prostration, were compelled to repeal their arbitrary acts within sixty days after their passage."

In another celebrated case in which Varnum took part, we have fortunately handed down to us a vivid description of the personality of the leading counsel, Hon. William Samuel Johnson, of Connecticut, and General Varnum.

It was the fashion of the bar of that day to be very well or elegantly dressed, and after describing Dr. Johnson's appearance, and his dress of black silk cut velvet, Mr. Updyke then describes the opposing counsel :

"Gen. Varnum appeared with his brick-colored coat, trimmed with gold lace, buckskin and small clothes, with gold lace knee bands, silk stockings and boots (Gen. Barton and himself being the only gentlemen who wore boots all day at that period), with a high, delicate and white forehead, with a cowlick on the right side ; eyes prominent and of a dark hue. His complexion was rather florid—somewhat corpulent, well proportioned and finely formed for strength and agility ; large eyebrows, nose straight and rather broad, teeth perfectly white, a profuse head of hair, short on the forehead, turned up some and deeply powdered and clubbed. When he took off his cocked hat he would lightly brush up his hair forward, while with a fascinating smile lighting up his countenance he took his seat in court opposite his opponent."

Mr. Wilkins Updyke in a personal letter to Hon. Benjamin F. Varnum (in the possession of his son John M. Varnum), dated in 1839, says :

"My eldest brother Daniel studied under General Varnum in 1784, and I have always been an ardent admirer of the character of the General * * * General Varnum was one of the most eloquent men that this or any other country ever produced. All the aged bear testimony unanimously as to his wonderful oratorical powers, and he was beloved by everybody. No one thought himself safe in a trial without him."

General Varnum became an original member of the Society of the Cincinnati on December 17, 1783, and was the first Vice President of the Rhode Island branch of that distinguished military order, and after the death of General Nathaniel Greene, succeeded the latter as President, a position which he retained until his death. He presided for the last time at the annual meeting held in the State House at Providence on the 4th July, 1787.

General Varnum was a warm and unwavering advocate for a federal constitution; he knew the inefficiency of the confederation, and the selfish considerations that governed the States, and felt that unless an instrument cementing the Union was speedily adopted, future efforts would be unavailing.

The following letter, dated August 24th, 1787, from him to Hon. Mr. Holton,—(probably Hon. Samuel Holton, a prominent member of Congress from Massachusetts)—gives General Varnum's views as to the proper form for a constitution. It will be noticed that the Constitution, as finally adopted after his death, followed substantially the lines suggested by him in this letter : *

"My worthy friend :

You have several times hinted the difficulty of expressing upon paper, ones ideas of an energetic federal government, altho' convinced of the inadequacy of our present system. Permit me to devote fifteen minutes to this subject ; and, as detail or amplification is unnecessary to an informed mind, I shall confine myself to principles.

These principles may be considered under two heads. The first as originating from the confederacy and directing the various powers that should be exercised by the nation collectively, and by the States individually.

The second, as flowing from the nature of civil Society having due regard to the customs, manners, laws, climates, religions, and pursuits of the citizens of the United States. Under this head may be considered the manner of exercising these powers, or the formal government of the Nation.

In the first place, whatever respect the citizens collectively, or as immediately relating to the whole confederacy, whether foreign or domestic, must be subjected to the national controul & whatever respects the citizens of a particular State, & has relation to them as such should be directed by the States respectively. But as interferences may sometimes arise

* This original letter is now in possession of Gen. James M. Varnum of New York.

the collective power must decide and enforce. This check would be better placed in the judiciary than the legislative branches.

In the second place, The Government of the United States should be so modified as to secure the rights of the different classes of citizens. But as these are distinguished by education, wealth & talents, they naturally divide into Aristocratical and Democratical. It is necessary then to form a Supreme legislative, perhaps as Congress is now formed, to originate all national laws, and submit them to the revision of a Senatorial body, which shall be formed out of equal districts of the United States, by the appointment of the Supreme legislative & whose commissions shall be so modified as to retain an equal number of old Members in office with the new, who may form a succession. In this body should reside the power of making war and peace.

The execution of the laws, both civil and military, should be placed in an executive council, consisting of a President of the United States, and the Officers of the great departments of War, Finance, Foreign Affairs, and Law, to be appointed by the Senate, & commissioned during good behavior, excepting the President, who should be appointed by both the legislative and senatorial bodies, & commissioned for a term of years, or for life. All appointments of Judges & other officers civil and military, should be made by the President, by and with advice of the council & commissioned in his name. These officers should be accountable for their conduct and triable before the respective tribunals before whom their actions would respectively be made cognizable. I think the President should not be liable to any direct prosecution as in him would reside that part of the sovereignty which displays itself in the etiquette of nations.

In this system, the balance would be secured, Military objects would be directed by the Senate, executed by the President and Council & checked by the fiscal power of the legislative.

The objects of revenue should be few, simple and well defined, & in case of very uncommon emergency, the States respectively should be called upon from contingents, which would form an ultimate and never failing check against encroachments upon the political system.

August 4th, 1787.

I am Sir, Yrs.

J. M. VARNUM.

Hon'ble Mr. Holton."

It would have been well if General Varnum could have been content to remain at his own comfortable home, with a wife whom he loved and cherished, in a state where he was at once a leader of the bar, and universally loved and respected and where all were proud to do him honor. But as a matter of fact, his health had become considerably impaired, and he had a tendency to weakness of the lungs, and the exposure of army life had implanted the seeds of pulmonary consumption in his system, which were aggravated by his constant laborious and strenuous work in his professional and in public affairs.

Varnum's judicial mind and public services, both in the army and Congress, had given him a reputation which extended throughout the whole country, and hence when the "Northwest Territory," a pet scheme of President Washington's, was formed (which included all the territory northwest of the Ohio) in 1787, Varnum was chosen as one of the Directors of the "Ohio Company of Associates" on August 29th, 1787; and on the 14th of October following, when General Arthur St. Clair was designated as Governor, General Varnum was appointed one of the United States Judges for that Territory, a position he accepted.

Accompanied only by Griffen Greene of Coventry, R. I., Varnum left his home in Rhode Island in the Spring of 1788, via Baltimore, and journeyed on horseback through the forests to Marietta, a town site selected by the New England Land Company at the junction of the Ohio and the Muskingum rivers. It is known that Varnum invested considerable money in the enterprise. The plans outlined partook of the methods of the speculative town boomers of the present age. The name finally selected was that of Queen Marie Antoinette, but the Roman classics were drawn upon in providing a Campus Martius, a via Sacra and a Capitolenum for the infant town. Malaria was prevalent and the location was a poor one in all respects.

He arrived at Marietta, Ohio, on June 5th, 1788, and at a celebration there on the 4th of July, was the orator of the day. Judge Varnum's oration was highly commended by all who heard it, and was subsequently published by the Directors of the Ohio Company, (Augt., 1788) copies of which are still extant, but extremely rare.

On the second day of July following, there being a quorum present (Generals Parsons, Varnum and Putnam), the Directors of the Ohio Company held their first meeting at Marietta, at which meeting, amongst other business transacted, was the change of the name of the city from Adelphia to Marietta.*

A grand celebration of the national holiday took place at Marietta on the fourth of July, 1788.

It is described as follows by Mr. Charles S. Hall in his interesting life of General Parsons : *

"There was a procession of the citizens and soldiery and a public dinner which was spread under a long bower built of intertwined oak and maple boughs near the North Point at the mouth of the Muskingum. The wealth of the rivers and forests was drawn upon to enrich the feast. Amongst the delicacies served was a pike weighing one hundred pounds. Patriotic toasts were given and an eloquent oration delivered by Judge Varnum.

Lamenting the absence of his Excellency Governor St. Clair 'upon this joyous occasion,' with uplifted hands he prays 'may he soon arrive,' and then turning first towards one and then towards the other, he thus apostrophizes the all unconscious rivers flowing on either side : 'Thou gentle flowing Ohio, whose surface as conscious of thy unequalled majesty, reflecteth no images but the grandeur of the impending heaven, bear him, oh ! bear him safely to this anxious spot ! And thou beautifully transparent Muskingum, swell at the moment of his approach, and reflect no objects but of pleasure and delight."

Thus in the fertile soil of Ohio, by a Rhode Island man, the first seeds of western eloquence were sown."

* Life and letters of Gen. S. H. Parsons, by C. S. Hall, Binghamton, N. Y., 1905-6.

One hundred and seven years later, on November 29th, 1905, a handsome bronze tablet was unveiled in the city of New York " to commemorate the great ordinance of 1787 establishing the Northwest Territory, and the sale of land to the Ohio Company of Associates."

The tablet is affixed to the portico of the United States Sub-Treasury in Wall Street, the site of Federal Hall, where the Congress met which enacted that ordinance. Upon it is an appropriate inscription, and in prominent letters also appear the following :

" Directors of the Ohio Company, 1787:

General Rufus Putnam	Rev. Manasseh Cutler
General Samuel Holden Parsons	General James Mitchell Varnum
Major Winthrop Sargent, Secretary	Colonel Richard Platt, Treasurer."

From the American Pioneer, Cincinnati, 1842, p. 64, we cull the following account of the opening of the United States Court for the Northwestern Territory :

" The first court held northwest of the Ohio River under the forms of court jurisprudence was opened at Campus Martius, Marietta, September 2d, 1788." * * *

On the preceding 7th of April, General Rufus Putnam, with forty-seven men, had landed and made the first permanent settlement, in what is now the State of Ohio. General Harmar with his regulars occupied Fort Harmar. Governor St. Clair and Generals Parsons and Varnum, Judges of the Supreme Court, arrived in July.

From a manuscript written by an eye witness, we have the following account of the ceremonies on this first opening of court :

" The procession was formed at the Point (where most of the settlers resided) in the following order :

1st   The High Sheriff, with his drawn sword.

2d   The citizens.

3d   The officers of the Garrison of Fort Harmar.

4th   The members of the Bar.

5th.   The Supreme Judges (Generals Varnum and Parsons).

6th   The Governor and clergyman.

7th   The newly appointed Judges of the Court of Common Pleas (Generals Rufus Putnam and Benjamin Tupper).

They marched up a path that had been cut and cleared through the forest to Campus Martius Hall (stockade) where the whole countermarched and the Judges took their seats.

After a blessing by the Rev. Dr. Cutler, the Sheriff Col. Ebenezer Sproat proclaimed with his solemn " Oyez " the opening of a court for the administration of even handed justice.

Although this scene was exhibited thus early in the settlement of the state, few ever equalled it in the dignity and the exalted character of principal participation. Many of them belong to the history of our country in the darkest as well as the most splendid periods of the Revolutionary War. To witness this spectacle, a large body of Indians was collected from the most powerful tribes, then occupying the almost entire west."

We learn from another source that the Indians were specially impressed by the commanding aspect and the piercing eyes of the High Sheriff, Colonel Sproat, and that they gave him the name of Hetuck, or "Buck-eye," from whence is derived the cognomen by which the state of Ohio and its residents have since become generally known.

Judge Varnum assisted Governor St. Clair and Judge Parsons in framing a code of laws for the territory, but this was his last official act, as his health which had been constantly declining since he left home rapidly became worse, and it became evident to all that the end was not far off.

It was about this time that Judge Varnum, who was supposed by many of his acquaintances to be if not an agnostic at least devoid of deep religious convictions, wrote the following touching and beautiful letter to his wife :

"Marietta, 18th December, 1788.

My dearest and most amiable friend:

I now write you from my sick chamber, and perhaps it will be the last letter that you will receive from me. My lungs are so far affected, that it is impossible for me to recover but by exchange of air and a warmer climate. I expect to leave this place on Sunday or Monday next for the falls of the Ohio. If I feel myself mend by the tour, I shall go no farther, but if not, and my strength should continue, I expect to proceed to New Orleans, and from thence to the West Indies & to Rhode Island. My physicians, most of them think the chances of recovery in my favor; however, I am neither elevated nor depressed by the force of opinion; but shall meet my fate with humility and fortitude.

I cannot however but indulge the hope, that I shall again embrace my lovely friend in this world, and that we may glide smoothly down the tide of time for a few years, and enjoy together the more substantial happiness and satisfaction as we have had already the desirable pleasures of life.

It is now almost nineteen years since Heaven connected us by the tenderest and the most sacred ties, and it is the same length of time that our friendship has been increased by every rational and endearing motive; it is now stronger than death, and I am firmly persuaded will follow us into an existence of never ending felicity.

But my lovely friend the gloomy moment will arrive when we must part; and should it arrive during our present separation, my last and only reluctant thoughts will be employed about my dearest Martha. Life, my dearest friend, is but a bubble, it soon bursts, and is remitted to eternity. When we look back to the earliest recollections of our youthful hours, it seems but the last period of our rest, and we appear to emerge from a night of slumbers to look forward to real existence. When we look forward time appears as indeterminate as eternity, and we have no idea of its termination but by the period of our dissolution. What particular relation it bears to a future state, our general notions of religion cannot point, we feel some things constantly active within us, that is evidently beyond the reach of mortality, but whether it is a part of ourselves, or an emanation from the pure source of existence or reabsorbed when death shall have finished his work, human wisdom cannot determine. Whether the demolition of the body introduces only a change in the manner of our being, or leaves it to progress infinitely, alternately elevated and depressed according to the propriety of our conduct, or whether we return to the common mass of unthinking matter, philosophy hesitates to decide.

I know therefore but one source from whence can be derived complete consolation in a dying hour, and that is the Divine system contained in the Gospel of Jesus Christ. There, life and immortality are brought to light; there, we are taught our existence is to be eternal. And secure in an interest in the atoning merits of a bleeding Saviour, that we shall be inconceivably happy. A firm and unshaken faith in this doctrine must raise us above the doubts and fears that hang upon every other system, and enable us to view with a calm serenity the approach of the King of Terrors, and to behold him as a kind and indulgent friend, spending his shafts only to carry us the sooner to our everlasting home. But should there be a more extensive religion beyond the veil, and without the reach of mortal observation, the Christian religion is by no means shaken thereby, and it is not opposed to any principle that admits of the perfect benevolence of deity. My only doubt is, whether the punishment threatened in the *New Testament* is annexed to a state of unbelief which may be removed hereafter, and so restoration take place, or whether the state of the mind at death irretrievably fixes its doom forever. I hope and pray that the divine spirit will give me such assurance of an acceptance with God, through the merits and sufferings of his Son, as to brighten the way to immediate happiness.

Dry up your tears, my charming mourner, nor suffer this letter to give too much inquietude. Consider the facts at present as in theory, but the sentiments such as will apply whenever the change shall come.

I know that humanity must and will be indulged in its keenest griefs, but there is no advantage in too deeply anticipating our inevitable sorrows. If I did not persuade myself that you would conduct with becoming prudence and fortitude, upon this occasion, my own unhappiness would be greatly increased, and perhaps my disorder too, but I have so much confidence in your discretion as to unbosom my inmost soul.

You must not expect to hear from me again until the coming Spring, as the river will soon be shut up with ice, and there will be no communication from below, and if in a situation for the purpose I will return as soon as practicable.

Give my sincerest love to all those you hold dear. I hope to see them again, and love them more than ever. Adieu, my dearest friend. And while I fervently devote in one undivided prayer, our immortal souls to the care, forgiveness, mercy and all prevailing grace of Heaven in time and through eternity, I must bid you a long, long, long farewell.

JAMES M. VARNUM."

On the 10th day of January, 1789, General Varnum passed away, at the Campus Martius at Marietta.

His remains were interred there with great solemnity and respect.

The following was the

ORDER OF PROCESSION.*

Marshals.

Mr. Wheaton, bearing the sword and military commission of the deceased on a mourning cushion.

Mr. Lord, bearing the civil commission on a mourning cushion.

Mr. Mayor, with the diploma and Order of the Cincinnati on a mourning cushion.

Mr. Fearing, with the insignia of Masonry on a mourning cushion.

Pall Supporters.	Corpse	*Pall Supporters.*
Griffin Greene,		Judge Crary,
Judge Tupper,		Judge Parsons,
William Sargeant, Esq.		Judge Putnam.
Private Mourners.		*Private Mourners.*
Mr. Charles Greene,		Mr. Richard Greene,
Mr. Frederic Crary,		Mr. Philip Greene,
Dr. Scott,		Dr. Tinley,
Deacon Story.		Dr. Drown.

Private Citizens.

Thirty Indian Chiefs.

Officers of Fort Harmer.

Civil Officers.

The Gentlemen of the Order of the Cincinnati.

Freemasons.

Mr. Clark, Mr. Stratton, Mr. Leach and Mr. Balch superintended the order of the procession, and the whole were preceded by Captain Zeigler

---

* Providence Gazette, March 7th, 1789.

of Fort Harmer with troops and music. A very affecting oration was delivered on the melancholy occasion (January 13th, 1789), by Dr. Solomon Drown.

This oration was subsequently published by the Ohio Company. It was reprinted in "The First Settlement of the Northwest Territory," a pamphlet published at Marietta in 1888.

General Varnum's burial place was on a ridge northeast of the mound near the stockade, but his remains, with those of a number of other officers, were many years afterwards removed to Oak Grove Cemetery, where they now rest.

We here quote again from Mr. Wilkins Updyke, who says :

"It might have been gratifying to his vanity, but Gen. Varnum committed an unfortunate error in accepting the office to which he was appointed. He had impaired his constitution by a free and liberal life, and with an enfeebled physical system, to leave his family, his circle of friends, and the comforts of an old State, and a delightful mansion erected in accordance to his own taste, and ornamented to his fancy, to become a kind of pioneer in a new and unsettled country, among strangers, and in a society uncongenial to his habits, was delusive—fatally delusive.

Professional pursuits, in our populous cities, are both more reputable and profitable than any of our national appointments. Yet the over-powering charm of being predistinguished from among the people as capable, or being selected from among our associates as entitled to public honor, is too alluring to individual vanity. But the abandonment of our country, our firesides, and the endearing connections of home, is a sacrifice too dear for it all. And so the unfortunate Varnum found it, on horseback, and attended by a solitary companion (Griffin Greene), he left a country that honored him, and an idolizing people, and traversed eight hundred miles of wilderness, mostly devoid of the comforts of life. And at his journey's end was tabernacled in a rude stockade, surrounded by excitements, his disorders aggravated for the want of retirement and repose, breathing the deadly exhalations of a great and sluggish river, and protected, by military array, from the incursions of the western savage. The issue proved he had no chance for life, and with a constitution too much impaired to return, he there lingered and expired."

Mr. Updyke concludes with the following epitome of General Varnum's career :

"The career of Gen. Varnum was active, but brief. He graduated at *twenty*, was admitted to the bar at *twenty-two*, entered the army at *twenty-seven*, resigned his commission at *thirty-one*, was member of Congress the same year, resumed his practice at *thirty-three*, continued his practice *four* years, was elected to Congress again at *thirty-seven*, emigrated to the West at *thirty-nine*, and died at the early age of *forty*. From the time of his admission to the bar to his departure from the state was *seventeen* years; deducting the *four* years he was in the military service, and *three* years he was in Congress, his actual professional life was only ten years."

*　　*　　*　　*

A century has passed since General Varnum delivered at Marietta the first oration ever delivered in this country in the territory northwest of the Ohio.

Once again, and on the seventh day of April, 1888, there is a celebration at Marietta, now in the great and flourishing state of Ohio, on the occasion of the centennial anniversary of the founding of the great Northwest. And again in an oration delivered, the orator of the day is the Honorable George Frisbie Hoar, a distinguished Senator of the United States from the state of Massachusetts, and his oration* is a magnificent tribute from posterity after the lapse of one hundred years, to the pioneers of 1788, and incidentally to the subject of this biographical sketch. We quote therefrom as follows :

"I do not believe the same number of persons fitted for the highest duties and responsibilities of war and peace could ever have been found in a community of the same size as were among the men who founded Marietta in the Spring of 1788. 　*　　*　　*
'I knew them all,' cried Lafayette, when the list of nearly fifty military officers who were among the pioneers was read to him at Marietta in 1825. 'I knew them all. I saw them at Brandywine, Yorktown and Rhode Island. They were the bravest of the brave.'

* Published by Charles Hamilton, Worcester, Mass., 1895. 6th edition.

Washington and Varnum, as well as Carrington and Lafayette, dwell chiefly, as was Washington's fashion, upon the personal quality of the men and not upon their public offices or titles. Indeed to be named with such commendation, upon personal knowledge, by the cautious and conscientious Washington, was to a veteran soldier better than being knighted on the field of battle.

* * * *

Your hearts are full of their memories. The stately figures of illustrious warriors and statesmen, the forms of sweet and comely matrons, living and real as if you had seen them yesterday, rise before us now," and amongst them "*Varnum*, than whom a courtlier figure never entered the presence of a queen — soldier, statesman, scholar, orator — of whom Thomas Paine, no mean judge, who had heard all the greatest English orators in the greatest days of English eloquence, declared the most eloquent man he had ever heard speak."

Notes to the foregoing biography of General James M. Varnum.

HIS MILITARY AND CIVIL COMMISSIONS.

The only one of these commissions now known to be in existence is that issued to him by William Greene, Governor, Captain General and Commander in Chief of the State of Rhode Island and Providence Plantation, as Major General of the State of Rhode Island, which bears date May 10th, 1779. It was under and by virtue of this commission that Varnum, although no longer in the Continental Army, acted in coöperation with the Comte de Rochambeau and his force in Rhode Island, during the later years of the war of the Revolution. This commission is now in the possession of General James M. Varnum of New York, the namesake and kinsman of the officer to whom it was issued.

HIS SWORD.

One of his swords is still in existence, and in excellent preservation. It is the same shown in the portrait of General Varnum, a copy of which appears in this volume.

His Will and Estate.

General Varnum by his will dated October 28, 1782, gave all his estate to his wife.

The will was admitted to probate at East Greenwich, May 30th, 1789, and his father in law Cromel Child was appointed his administrator.

The inventory shows that his personal estate was small — less than £300.

Books of Reference.

Memoirs of the Rhode Island Bar, by Wilkins Updyke, Providence. (Contains a long and interesting Biography.)

Register of the Society of the Cincinnati in Rhode Island, by Asa Bird Gardiner. (In press.)

General James M. Varnum of the Continental Army, by Asa Bird Gardiner (James M. Varnum collaborating). " Magazine of American History," Sept., 1887.

The case of Trevett against Weeden, by James M. Varnum, Esq., Major-General of the State of Rhode Island, &c., Counsellor at law and Member of Congress for said State. Providence—Printed by John Carter, 1787. (Copy in possession of James M. Varnum of New York.)

Oration, delivered at Marietta, July 4th, 1788, by the Hon. James M. Varnum, Esq., one of the Judges of the Western Territory, &c. Newport, R. I. Printed by Peter Edes, 1788. (Copy in possession of James M. Varnum, of New York.)

Oration of Dr. Solomon Drown at the funeral of General Varnum at Marietta on January 13th, 1789. (Original in possession of Henry R. Drowne, Esq., of New York.)

Oration of Dr. Solomon Drown at Marietta, April 7th, 1789, containing allusion to General Varnum. Worcester, Mass. Isaiah Thomas, 1789.

Memorial of James Mitchel Varnum. His Publick Services and Excerpt from his Diary of Events. Printed for subscribers. Providence, 1792. (This book is referred to and quoted from in " Paul Jones, Founder of the American Navy." Mr. Buell, the editor, made these extracts in 1886, but the compilers of this work have been unable after diligent inquiry to find a copy.)

www.ingramcontent.com/pod-product-compliance
Lightning Source LLC
Chambersburg PA
CBHW030911260626
47169CB00008B/2788